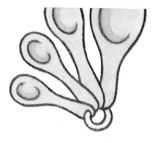

A NOTE TO PARENTS

Early Step into Reading Books are designed for preschoolers and kindergartners who are just getting ready to read. The words are easy, the type is big, and the stories are packed with rhyme, rhythm, and repetition.

We suggest that you read this book to your child the first few times, pointing to each word as you go. Soon your child will start saying the words with you. And before long, he or she will try to read the story alone. Don't be surprised if your child uses the pictures to figure out the text—that's what they're there for! The important thing is to develop your child's confidence—and to show your child that reading is fun.

When your child is ready to move on, try the rest of the steps in our Step into Reading series. **Step 1 Books** (preschool–grade 1) feature the same easy-to-read type as the Early Step into Reading Books, but with more words per page. **Step 2 Books** (grades 1–3) are both longer and slightly more difficult, while **Step 3 Books** (grades 2–3) introduce readers to paragraphs and fully developed plot lines. **Step 4 Books** (grades 2–4) offer exciting nonfiction for the increasingly independent reader.

The grade levels assigned to the five steps are intended only as guides. Some children move through all five steps very rapidly; others climb the steps over a period of several years. Either way, these books will help your child "step into reading" in style!

Library of Congress Cataloging-in-Publication Data
Trimble, Irene.
Ord eats a pizza! / by Irene Trimble ; illustrated by Peter Panas.
 p. cm. — (Early step into reading)
SUMMARY: Emmy, Zak, Cassie, Max, and Ord have very different ideas about how to make a pizza.
ISBN 0-375-81085-4 (trade) — ISBN 0-375-91085-9 (lib. bdg.)
[1. Pizza—Fiction. 2. Puppets—Fiction. 3. Stories in rhyme.]
I. Panas, Peter, ill. II. Title. III. Series. PZ8.3.T6943 Or 2000 [E]—dc21 00-029242

Printed in the United States of America November 2000 10 9 8 7 6 5 4

www.randomhouse.com/kids/sesame
Visit Dragon Tales on the Web at www.dragontales.com

Early Step into Reading™

Ord Eats a Pizza!

By Irene Trimble

Illustrated by Peter Panas

Based on the characters by Ron Rodecker

I wish, I wish
With all my heart
To fly with dragons
In a land apart.

Random House New York

Max loves pizza.
It must be grand.
So, let's make one
in Dragon Land!

Mix it.

Twirl it.

Toss it high!

What goes on
a pizza pie?

9

Zak says,

"Horseflies go on top,
with earmuffs, drums,
and green gumdrops!"

11

Wheezie says,
"No, a flute and horn,
with fairy shoes
and pink popcorn!"

Horseflies, flutes,
and horns? Oh, my!
Is this what goes
on pizza pie?

Let's ask Cassie!
She might know
what goes best
on pizza dough.

Cassie knows

just who to ask.

Max loves pizza.

"Hey!" says Max.

"We <u>all</u> can make it."

"These go on top."

"Then you bake it!"

And in the blink
of a dragon's eye,
they make a dragon
pizza pie!

Good job, Emmy,
Wheezie, Zak!
Good job, Cassie…

Ord and Max!